Dear Parents and Educators,

Welcome to Penguin Young Readers! As parents and educators, you know that each child develops at his or her own pace—in terms of speech, critical thinking, and, of course, reading. Penguin Young Readers recognizes this fact. As a result, each Penguin Young Readers book is assigned a traditional easy-to-read level (1–4) as well as a Guided Reading Level (A–P). Both of these systems will help you choose the right book for your child. Please refer to the back of each book for specific leveling information. Penguin Young Readers features esteemed authors and illustrators, stories about favorite characters, fascinating nonfiction, and more!

Angelina Ballerina™: Angelina Takes a Bow

LEVEL 2

GUIDED READING LEVEL **H**

This book is perfect for a **Progressing Reader** who:
• can figure out unknown words by using picture and context clues;
• can recognize beginning, middle, and ending sounds;
• can make and confirm predictions about what will happen in the text; and
• can distinguish between fiction and nonfiction.

Here are some **activities** you can do during and after reading this book:
• Retelling: Use your memory to tell what the ballet is about. What happens in the beginning, middle, and end? Who are the main characters?
• Make Connections: By the end of the story, Angelina realizes that her part in the ballet is important—even if she isn't always dancing. Together, all the dancers tell a wonderful story. Can you think of a time when a small thing you did made a much bigger difference than you thought it would?

Remember, sharing the love of reading with a child is the best gift you can give!

—Bonnie Bader, EdM
  Penguin Young Readers program

*Penguin Young Readers are leveled by independent reviewers applying the standards developed by Irene Fountas and Gay Su Pinnell in *Matching Books to Readers: Using Leveled Books in Guided Reading*, Heinemann, 1999.

HiT entertainment

Penguin Young Readers
Published by the Penguin Group
Penguin Group (USA) Inc., 375 Hudson Street, New York, New York 10014, USA
Penguin Group (Canada), 90 Eglinton Avenue East, Suite 700,
Toronto, Ontario M4P 2Y3, Canada
(a division of Pearson Penguin Canada Inc.)
Penguin Books Ltd., 80 Strand, London WC2R 0RL, England
Penguin Group Ireland, 25 St. Stephen's Green, Dublin 2, Ireland
(a division of Penguin Books Ltd.)
Penguin Group (Australia), 250 Camberwell Road, Camberwell, Victoria 3124, Australia
(a division of Pearson Australia Group Pty. Ltd.)
Penguin Books India Pvt. Ltd., 11 Community Centre, Panchsheel Park,
New Delhi—110 017, India
Penguin Group (NZ), 67 Apollo Drive, Rosedale, Auckland 0632, New Zealand
(a division of Pearson New Zealand Ltd.)
Penguin Books (South Africa) (Pty.) Ltd., 24 Sturdee Avenue,
Rosebank, Johannesburg 2196, South Africa

Penguin Books Ltd., Registered Offices: 80 Strand, London WC2R 0RL, England

ISBN 978-0-448-45618-8   10 9 8 7 6 5 4 3 2

PENGUIN YOUNG READERS

LEVEL **2**

PROGRESSING READER

Angelina Takes a Bow

inspired by the classic children's book series
by author Katharine Holabird
and illustrator Helen Craig

Penguin Young Readers
An Imprint of Penguin Group (USA) Inc.

Angelina has exciting news.

"Mom! Polly!" she calls out.

"I'm going to be the prima

ballerina in the school ballet!"

"What's a prima ballerina?" Polly asks

"It means I get to dance the

most," Angelina tells Polly.

"And when I take my bow,

I'll get the most cheers!"

At school, Ms. Mimi tells the

dancers about the ballet.

The prima ballerina is

a fairy named Fern.

Fern is the best dancer

in the magic forest.

This is Angelina's part.

A.Z. is going to play the part

of the Elf Prince.

In the ballet, the Elf Prince

likes Fern's dancing.

He gives her many gifts.

But one of the other

fairies is mad.

She wants gifts from the

Elf Prince, too.

So the mean fairy gives

Fern a magic pillow.

Fern falls asleep, never

to dance again!

Oh no! Angelina does not want
to sleep—she wants to dance!

Angelina asks Ms. Mimi if she

can play another part.

Ms. Mimi tells Angelina that if she wants to she can switch parts *after* the first rehearsal.

At the first rehearsal, everyone

dances except Angelina.

Will I ever get to dance?

Angelina thinks sadly.

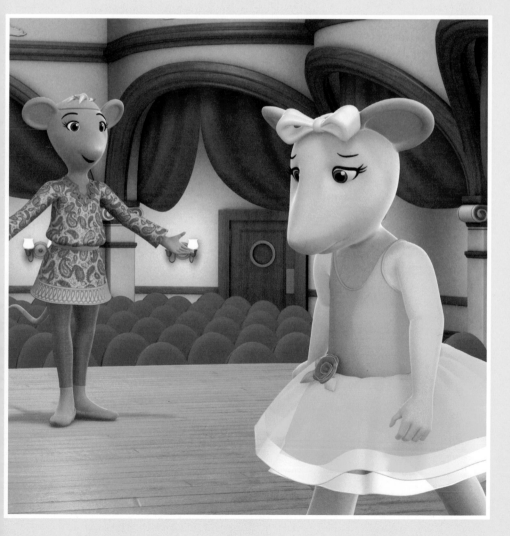

Finally it is Angelina's

turn to shine!

But as soon as she starts

to dance, the music changes.

Oh no! It is the mean fairy.

She gives Angelina a magic pillow.

Ms. Mimi tells Angelina that

Fern has to fall asleep before her

friends can break the spell.

"You mean Fern is going

to wake up?" Angelina asks.

"Maybe I will get to

dance after all!"

Angelina puts her head

on the pillow.

She pretends to fall asleep.

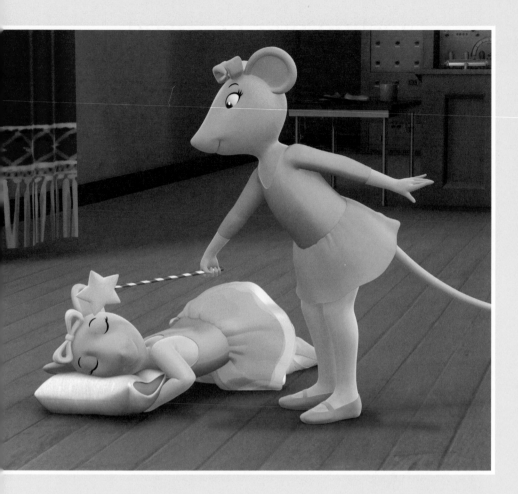

Alice taps Angelina with

her magic wand.

"Now what?" Angelina whispers.

"Now you dance!" says Ms. Mimi.

"I slept and slept and slept,"
Angelina says.

"But now I get to dance
and dance and dance!"

29

Angelina realizes that her

part is important.

Her friends' parts are

important, too.

Together they tell a wonderful story.

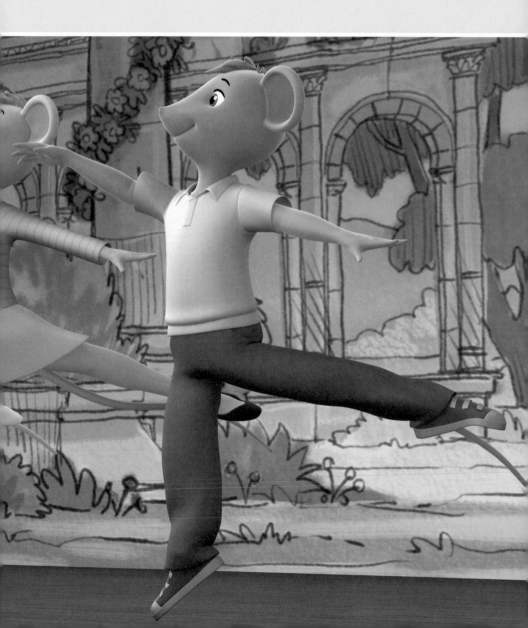

Angelina takes a bow.

What a nice ballet!